GOD LOVES ME
BIBLE

Written by Susan Elizabeth Beck
Illustrated by Lisa Mallett

ZONDER**kidz**

ZONDERVAN.com/
AUTHORTRACKER
follow your favorite authors

ZONDERKIDZ

God Loves Me Bible
Copyright © 2004 by Zonderkidz
Illustrations © 2013 by Lisa Mallett

Requests for information should be addressed to:

Zonderkidz, 5300 Patterson Ave SE, Grand Rapids, Michigan 49530

ISBN 978-0-310-73398-0

Editors: Barbara Herndon, Catherine DeVries, Jean Syswerda
Art direction and design: Kris Nelson

Printed in China

16 17 18 19 20 / DSC / 23 22 21 20 19 18 17 16 15 14 13 12 11 10 9 8 7 6 5 4 3 2

THE BEGINNING

CREATION

In the beginning there was nothing.

Then God made the sky and the earth.

God made the sun and the stars.

God made the water and the land.
He made the fish and the birds and all
the animals. He put them on the earth.

God loved his world.

And God loves **me!**

ADAM & EVE

God made two people
to take care of his world.
He made a man named Adam
and a woman named Eve.
Adam and Eve lived in a beautiful
place called the Garden of Eden.

God loved Adam and Eve.

And God loves **me!**

NOAH

Noah was God's friend.
God told Noah to build a big boat
because a flood was coming. Noah
listened to God. Noah built the boat.
Then he put his family in the boat and
many animals too. When the terrible
flood came, Noah and his family and
the animals were safe inside the boat.

God loved Noah and his family
and the animals.

And God loves **me!**

God loved

the world,
Adam and Eve,
Noah and
his family,
and the animals.

Do you know who else God loves?

Me!

MORE PEOPLE
on the Earth

ABRAHAM

God chose Abraham
to be the father of a special nation
of people. God promised Abraham
as many children as there
are stars in the sky.

God loved Abraham.

And God loves **me!**

SARAH

Sarah was very, very old.
God told her she would have a baby.
Sarah laughed. An old lady
couldn't have a baby! But God
gave Sarah and Abraham a son.
They named him Isaac.

God loved Sarah.

And God loves **me!**

ISAAC

Isaac was Abraham and Sarah's only child. As a test, God told Abraham to sacrifice Isaac. Abraham was very, very sad. But he was willing to obey God. Abraham passed God's test. God sent a ram and Abraham sacrificed it instead. God promised to make their family into a great nation.

God loved Isaac.

And God loves **me!**

REBEKAH

Rebekah was a very beautiful girl.
She was kind and she was brave.
Rebekah left her family and moved
far away. She married Isaac, and
Isaac loved her. Rebekah became the
mother of twin boys: Jacob and Esau.

God loved Rebekah.

And God loves **me!**

JACOB

Jacob had a dream.
He saw a stairway going up to heaven.
Angels were walking up and down
the stairway. God stood at the very top.
God spoke to Jacob. He promised
Jacob a lot of land and many children.
God promised never to leave Jacob.

God loved Jacob.

And God loves **me!**

RACHEL

Rachel was a beautiful girl.
She took care of her father's sheep.
She married Jacob, and he loved her.
Rachel had two sons:
Joseph and Benjamin.

God loved Rachel.

And God loves **me!**

JOSEPH

Joseph's father loved him
very much. He gave Joseph a
colorful robe. But Joseph's brothers
didn't like him. They sent Joseph
far from home. But God kept
Joseph safe. He made Joseph
a great man in Egypt.

God loved Joseph.

And God loves **me!**

God loved

Abraham and Sarah,
Isaac and Rebekah,
Jacob and Rachel,
Joseph,
and all the people
God had created.

Do you know who else God loves?

Me!

God's Special People
THE
ISRAELITES

THE BABY
MOSES

Moses' mother was a slave
in Egypt. She hid him from the soldiers.
The soldiers were trying to hurt Moses
and other Hebrew baby boys. She put
baby Moses in a basket and placed it in
the Nile River. A princess found Moses.
She kept him safe from the soldiers.

God loved baby Moses.

And God loves **me!**

THE LEADER
MOSES

Moses talked with God.
God spoke to Moses from a
burning bush. God told Moses
to help his people the Israelites.
Moses became a great
leader of God's people.

God loved the leader Moses.

And God loves **me!**

THE
ISRAELITE
SLAVES

God's people lived in Egypt.
They worked very hard for the king.
They were unhappy, so they prayed
to God. God sent Moses to ask the king
to let the people go. But the king said,
"No!" Then God sent terrible plagues—
frogs and grasshoppers and boils
and flies. There were ten plagues in all.
Then the king let God's people go.

God loved the Israelite slaves.

And God loves **me!**

MIRIAM

Miriam was Moses' sister.
She left Egypt with him and
all God's people. God parted the
waters of the Red Sea so they could
walk across on dry land. When Miriam
reached the other side, she danced and
sang a special song of thanks to God.

God loved Miriam.

And God loves **me!**

THE
HUNGRY
ISRAELITES

God's people took a long trip
in the desert. They became very
hungry. God sent special bread
from heaven every morning
to cover the ground.
The people called the bread manna.

God loved his people, the Israelites.

And God loves **me!**

MOSES
CLIMBS A MOUNTAIN

God told Moses to climb
a mountain. Moses was up there
for a long time. God gave Moses
ten rules for the people to follow.
These rules are called
the Ten Commandments.

God loved Moses.

And God loves **me!**

CALEB & JOSHUA

Twelve men went to explore
the promised land of Canaan.
Ten of the men were scared and said
God's people should not go there.
But Caleb and Joshua thought
the land was wonderful.
They knew God would help
his people conquer Canaan.

● ● ● ● ● ❀ ● ● ● ●

God loved Caleb and Joshua.

And God loves **me!**

JOSHUA

Joshua was a great leader.
He led God's people to the
promised land. Joshua's army
conquered the city of Jericho.
God told them to march around
the city. He told them to shout and
blow trumpets. Then God made
the walls of Jericho fall down.

God loved Joshua.

And God loves **me!**

God loved

Moses and Miriam
and
Caleb and Joshua
and
God's special people,
the Israelites.

Do you know who else God loves?

Me!

God's People in the
PROMISED LAND

DEBORAH

Deborah was a prophet
and a judge. She trusted God.
She helped people stop fighting.
When an enemy came to attack,
Deborah showed Barak and his army
how to defeat them. God's people won!
Deborah wrote a beautiful
song of thanks to God.

God loved Deborah.

And God loves **me!**

SAMSON

God made Samson strong and special. When Samson was young, he obeyed God. But when he grew up, he did not always obey God. But God still used Samson as a leader of God's people.

God loved Samson.

And God loves **me!**

RUTH

Ruth was sad. Her husband had died.
She had no children, but she loved
her husband's mother, Naomi.
Ruth promised never to leave Naomi.
She promised to love Naomi's
God and her people.
God blessed Ruth. He gave her
a new husband and a son.

God loved Ruth.

And God loves **me!**

SAMUEL

When Samuel was a little boy,
he lived in the temple.
One night he heard a voice calling
his name—one, two, three times.
When the voice called again,
Samuel said, "Here I am, Lord."
Samuel listened to God.
He obeyed God all of his life.

God loved Samuel.

And God loves **me!**

God loved

Deborah
and Samson
and Ruth
and Samuel
and all God's people
in the promised land.

Do you know who else God loves?

Me!

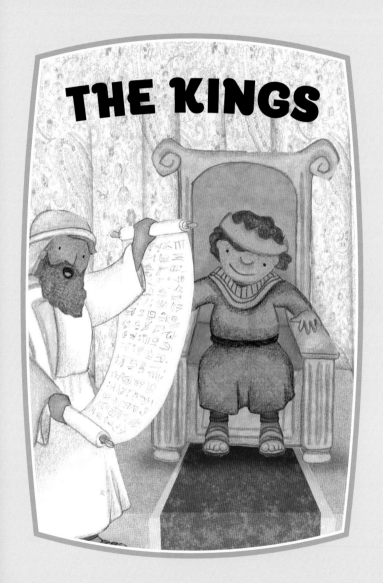

THE KINGS

SAUL

God had chosen Saul to be king of
Israel. Saul was taller than the other
men in Israel. But Saul was shy.
He hid when the people wanted
to make him king. But the people
found him. They put a crown on
his head, and they made Saul
the first king of Israel.

God loved Saul.

And God loves **me!**

THE SHEPHERD BOY
DAVID

David was a shepherd.
He took good care of his father's
sheep. He was strong and brave.
When a lion and a bear attacked
the sheep, David saved the sheep.

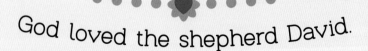

God loved the shepherd David.

And God loves **me!**

THE FIGHTER
DAVID

David was too young to
join the army. But one day
he fought the enemy all alone!
He fought a giant named Goliath.
David was much smaller than Goliath,
and Goliath called him names.
But David trusted God, and he won!

God loved the fighter David.

And God loves **me!**

JONATHAN

Jonathan was the son of King Saul.
Jonathan was best friends with David.
He shot arrows with David in the fields.
Jonathan protected David
when King Saul was angry.

God loved Jonathan.

And God loves **me!**

KING DAVID

David was the youngest boy
in his family. No one
thought he could be a king.
But God chose David to be a
great and powerful king.

God loved King David.

And God loves **me!**

SOLOMON

Solomon was a good and fair king of Israel. He asked God to make him wise. God gave Solomon his wish. God also made Solomon very rich. Solomon built a beautiful temple for God in Jerusalem.

God loved Solomon.

And God loves **me!**

JOASH

God's temple needed fixing.
Joash was the king of Judah.
He wanted to make God's temple a
beautiful place again. The people gave
Joash a lot of money to pay for the
work. Joash gave the money to the
workers who fixed up God's temple.
Joash was a good king.

God loved Joash.

And God loves **me!**

JOSIAH

Josiah was a little boy
when he became king of Israel.
He was only eight years old!
One day the priests found some
very old books in the temple.
Josiah told the priests to read the
books to the people. The people loved
to hear what God said in the books.

God loved Josiah.

And God loves **me!**

God
loved

Saul
and David
and Jonathan
and Solomon
and all the kings
of his nation.

Do you know who else God loves?

Me!

THE PROPHETS

THE PROPHET
ELIJAH

Elijah loved God
and obeyed him.
When there was no food
to eat, God sent birds
to bring food to Elijah.

• • • • ❤ • • • •

God loved the prophet Elijah.

And God loves **me!**

ELIJAH
GOES TO HEAVEN

One day Elijah took a walk
with his friend Elisha.
Suddenly a chariot and horses of
fire flew between Elijah and Elisha.
Then a whirlwind came and picked
Elijah up and carried him to heaven.

God loved Elijah.

And God loves **me!**

ISAIAH

God needed someone to bring
news to his people, the Israelites.
God asked Isaiah to be his messenger.
At first, Isaiah was afraid.
He didn't think he could do the job.
But then he said, "Here I am.
Send me." Isaiah became a great
messenger of God to the Israelites.

God loved Isaiah.

And God loves **me!**

JONAH

God told Jonah to go to Nineveh.
But Jonah didn't listen.
He got on a ship and sailed away.
When a storm came, Jonah
was thrown into the sea.
A big fish swallowed Jonah.
Jonah prayed to God,
and God saved him.

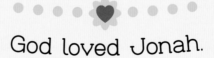

God loved Jonah.

And God loves **me!**

God
loved

Elijah
and Isaiah
and Jonah
and all his messengers.

Do you know who else God loves?

Me!

GOD'S PEOPLE
Away from Home

THREE
BRAVE MEN

Shadrach, Meshach, and Abednego
were taken far away to a country
called Babylon. The king wanted
them to worship a golden statue.
But the three men loved God.
They would not worship anything else.
So the king threw them into a fire.
It was very, very hot. But the three men
did not get burned. God kept them safe.

God loved Shadrach, Meshach, and Abednego

And God loves **me!**

DANIEL

Every day Daniel prayed to God.
One day the king said,
"No one may pray to God."
But Daniel prayed anyway.
The king ordered the soldiers
to throw Daniel into a den of lions.
But God kept Daniel safe.
The lions did not hurt him.
Daniel trusted and obeyed God.

God loved Daniel.

And God loves **me!**

ESTHER

Esther became the queen of
a great nation. A wicked man made
a plan to kill all of the Israelites.
When Esther found out about the plan,
she told the king. Esther trusted God,
and God's people were saved.

God loved Esther.

And God loves **me!**

EZRA

Ezra lived in Babylon.
He was a teacher. He studied God's
rules. One day the king told him he
could go back home to Israel.
Ezra led many, many people back
to the city of Jerusalem. With the help
of the people, Ezra rebuilt God's temple.

God loved Ezra.

And God loves **me!**

God loved

Daniel
and Esther
and Ezra
and all God's people
who were far away
from home.

Do you know who else God loves?

Me!

JESUS
Comes to Earth

MARY

Mary was a young girl who
loved God. One day an angel
came to Mary. The angel told Mary
that she would have a baby boy.
The baby would be God's Son,
and his name would be Jesus.
Mary was a wonderful mother.

God loved Mary.

And God loves **me!**

JOSEPH

Joseph was a carpenter.
He loved Mary very much,
and he planned to marry her.
An angel told Joseph that Mary was
going to have a baby—God's Son.
Joseph took good care of Mary
and the baby Jesus.

God loved Joseph.

And God loves **me!**

THE
BABY JESUS

Jesus was a very special baby.
He was born in a stable in Bethlehem.
Angels appeared to shepherds
and told them that Jesus was born.
A very bright star sparkled in the sky.
Wise Men followed the star from far
away to see Jesus and bring him gifts.
Jesus was the Son of God.

● ● ● ● ✿ ● ● ● ●

God loved the baby Jesus.

And God loves **me!**

THE
BOY JESUS

Jesus was twelve years old when he went to the temple in Jerusalem with Mary and Joseph. When it was time to go home, Jesus stayed in the temple. He listened to the teachers there and asked many questions. All the people were amazed at how smart Jesus was.

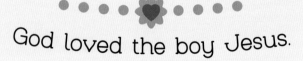

God loved the boy Jesus.

And God loves **me!**

JOHN
THE BAPTIST

John the Baptist was a preacher. He lived in the desert. His clothes were made of camel hair, and he ate bugs and honey. John told the people that Jesus was coming to save them from their sins. John baptized many people in the Jordan River.

God loved John the Baptist.

And God loves **me!**

GOD'S SON
JESUS

Jesus came to John the Baptist
to be baptized in the Jordan River.
When Jesus came out of the river,
a dove landed on his shoulder.
A voice from heaven said,
"This is my Son, and I love him."

God loved his Son, Jesus.

And God loves **me!**

God loved

Mary and Joseph,
John the Baptist,
and Jesus
when he was a baby,
when he was a little boy,
and when he
was grown up.

Do you know who else God loves?

Me!

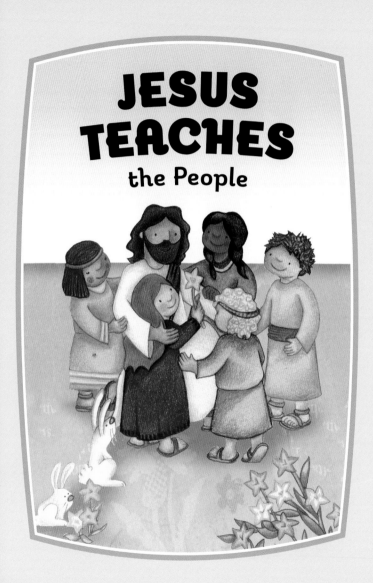

JESUS TEACHES
the People

THE TWELVE
DISCIPLES

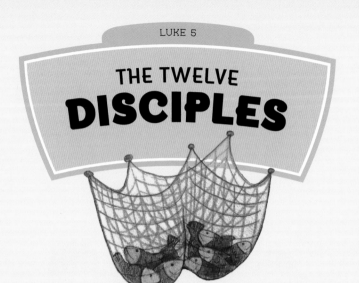

Jesus had twelve special friends.
They were called his disciples.
The disciples were ordinary people.
Jesus chose them to tell
others about God.

God loved the twelve disciples.

And God loves **me!**

A VERY SICK
LITTLE GIRL

Jairus had a little daughter.
She was very sick. Jairus went to
Jesus for help. Jesus came to their
house. Everyone was crying
because the little girl was dead.
Then Jesus did something wonderful!
He took the little girl by the hand
and made her alive again!

God loved the little girl.

And God loves **me!**

MARY & MARTHA

Mary and Martha were friends of Jesus. One day Martha got angry because Mary listened to Jesus instead of helping in the kitchen. But Jesus told Martha that Mary had chosen the right thing.

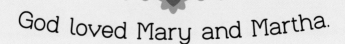

God loved Mary and Martha.

And God loves **me!**

THE LITTLE
CHILDREN

Some people brought their
children to see Jesus.
They wanted Jesus to touch
them and pray for them.
The little children were very
special to Jesus. He talked to them.
He gave them hugs!

God loved the little children.

And God loves **me!**

ZACCHAEUS

Zacchaeus was a very short man who wasn't very nice. He climbed a tree so he could see Jesus as he walked by. Jesus stopped to talk to Zacchaeus. Then Jesus ate supper with him. Zacchaeus promised to be nice.

God loved Zacchaeus.

And God loves **me!**

THE
RISEN JESUS

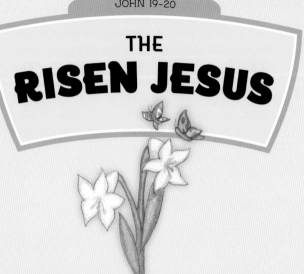

Jesus knew God sent him
to earth to die for everyone's sins.
But Jesus did not stay dead.
He came out of his grave
three days later,
just like he said he would!

God loved his Son, Jesus.

And God loves **me!**

JESUS
GOES TO HEAVEN

After Jesus rose from the dead,
he taught his disciples
many more good things.
Then Jesus went up into heaven.
He disappeared behind a cloud.
His disciples were all alone.
Two angels appeared. They promised
that Jesus would come to earth again!

God loved his Son, Jesus.

And God loves **me!**

God loved

Mary and Martha
and
Zacchaeus
and
all the people
Jesus knew on earth.

Do you know who else God loves?

Me!

Yes,
God loves
ME!

INDEX

The Prophets

God's People Away From Home

Jesus Comes to Earth

Jesus Teaches the People

We want to hear from you. Please send your comments about this book to us in care of zreview@zondervan.com. Thank you.

ZONDERVAN.com/
AUTHORTRACKER
follow your favorite authors